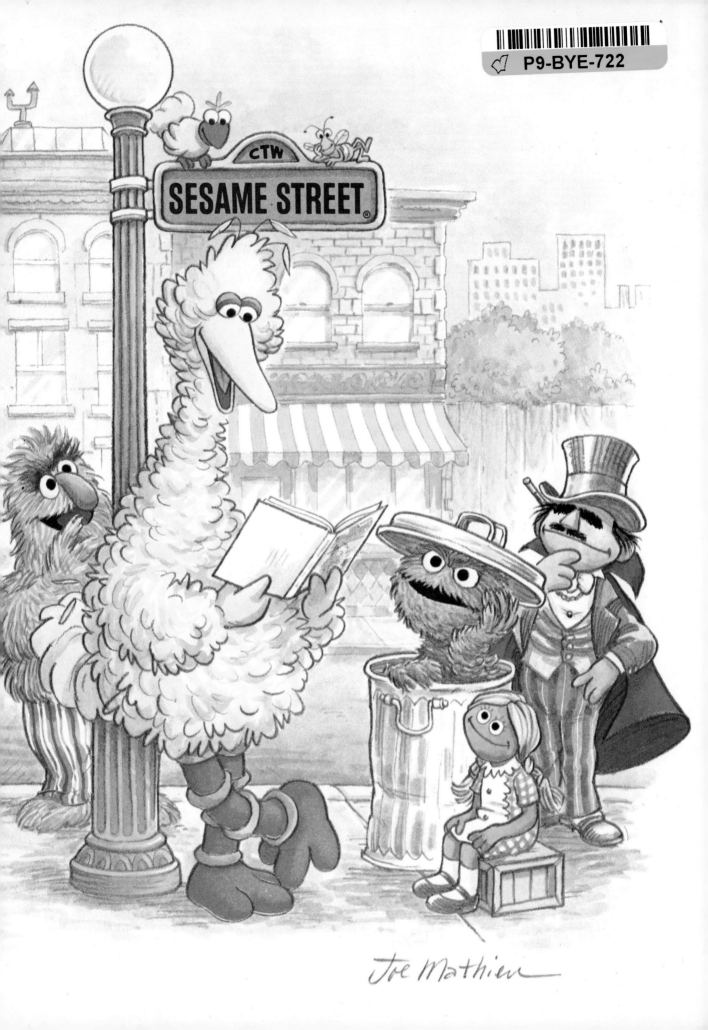

THE SESAME STREET® LIBRARY

With Jim Henson's Muppets

VOLUME 11

FEATURING
THE LETTERS
U AND V
AND THE NUMBER
11

Children's Television Workshop/Funk & Wagnalls, Inc.

WRITTEN BY:

Michael Frith
Emily Perl Kingsley
David Korr
Sharon Lerner
Nina B. Link
Jeffrey Moss
Norman Stiles
Daniel Wilcox

ILLUSTRATED BY:

Mel Crawford
Peter Cross
A. Delaney
Michael Frith
Joseph Mathieu
Jon McIntosh
Michael J. Smollin
Caroll Spinney

PHOTOGRAPHS BY:

Charles P. Rowan

Once Upon an Eleven

ERNIE PRESENTS THE LETTER U

King Marvin the Magnificent was very grand indeed.
He said, "I am magnificent." His subjects all agreed.
"King Marvin is magnificent! Our kingdom is most blest.
Of all the Kings who ever were, King Marvin is the best."

Now in King Marvin's kingdom lived a little boy named Paul
Whose favorite thing was playing with a bright pink rubber ball.
He bounced his rubber ball all day against the palace gate.
He started in the morning and he stayed till it grew late.

One day as he was playing ball, he stopped and said, "I know!
I think I'll throw my rubber ball as high as it will go."
So Paul wound up and threw the ball with one tremendous fling.
"Oh, no!" he cried. "It's headed for the window of the King!"

Smash! went the royal window,
and before the King could duck,
The ball bounced off
King Marvin's throne . . .

and hit his nose . . .

and stuck.

"What *is* this thing?" said Marvin
    as he felt the ball and sneered.
But before he could remove it,
    his Prime Minister appeared.

"King Marv!" cried the Prime Minister.
    "A rubber ball! How cute!
    It really is magnificent! I'll get one for *my* snoot."

And like a flash he left the room, and what do you suppose?
When he returned, a rubber ball was stuck upon *his* nose.

The news spread quickly through the land
(the kingdom was quite small).
Soon on each person's nose there was
a bright pink rubber ball.

The butcher and the baker and the driver of the bus
All said, "If Marvin likes it, then it's good enough for us."

"Don't we look great!" the people cried.
        "Our noses are so pleasing!
Except it's rather hard to smell, and even harder sneezing."

But everyone was happy, the whole kingdom filled with joy,
For everybody had a ball—except for one small boy.

"Oh, woe," cried Paul, "without my ball
        I really am so sad.
I'll ask the King to give it back—
        I hope he won't be mad."

Paul tiptoed to the throne room
     where King Marvin was alone.
The King in his magnificence
     sat on his royal throne.

Young Paul knelt down before the King
     and then was told to rise,
But when he lifted up his head
     a strange sight met his eyes.
King Marvin wore an ermine cloak,
     silk slippers on his toes,
A golden crown was on his head . . .
     and a ball was on his nose.

Then Paul began to giggle, and he laughed till he was sore,
And pretty soon he laughed so hard, he fell down on the floor.

"What's so funny?" said King Marvin,
    as he saw that Paul was staring.
"It's your nose!" cried Paul with laughter.
    "That's my favorite toy you're wearing."

    "My nose looks great!" King Marvin said.
    Said Paul, "I beg to differ.
    You really do look silly
    with that ball stuck on your sniffer."

    "I do?" exclaimed King Marvin.
    "Bring my royal mirror quick."
    King Marvin looked. He saw himself,
    and what he said was…"Ick!"

    "I really do look silly,
    and I knew it from the first.
    I've always said that rubber balls
    on noses are the worst!"

The King took off the rubber ball and handed it to Paul.
"You've taught me a great lesson,
    so I'll give you back your ball."
Then the butcher and the baker and the driver of the bus
Said, "If Marvin gave his ball away...
                    that's good enough for us!"

The people of the kingdom gave their rubber balls away
And they all have worn their noses plain...
                    ... right to this very day.

So from early in the morning time until it grows quite late,
Paul has a hundred balls to bounce against the palace gate.

Now this story has a moral
And it's very, very true—
If a king does something silly
You don't have to do it too.

Thumbelina

Once there was a girl called Thumbelina who was only as big as your thumb. She was so pretty that everyone wanted to marry her.

One night while Thumbelina slept, an ugly old toad picked her up and carried her off. The toad wanted Thumbelina to marry her wicked toad son.

But Thumbelina ran away and a kindly mouse took her in. A few days later the mouse took Thumbelina to see Mr. Mole's dark home underground. As soon as he saw the tiny girl, he wanted to marry Thumbelina. He was so kind that she said she would marry him. But to tell the truth, she really didn't love the idea of living underground.

Just one month before the wedding, Thumbelina found a dying swallow in the meadow. She nursed the poor swallow back to health and one day while taking care of him she said, "How I wish I could fly away like you."

When the swallow was better, he told Thumbelina to climb onto his back. Together they flew away to the Land of the Flowers, where Thumbelina met the Flower King. He, too, was only as big as your thumb. Before long they had fallen in love. Thumbelina was happy at last.

Then it cracks open
the cocoon and flies away.
This cracked cocoon means
that Clarence is now a butterfly!
I, Sherlock Hemlock, have solved
another case! Why, young man,
why are you crying again?

Oh, Mr. Detective!
Clarence, my pet
butterfly, is missing!
Whatever shall I do?

Never fear! I, Sherlock Hemlock,
will solve the case.
Pardon me, sir. Is your name Clarence?
Excuse me, madam. Are you Clarence?
I beg your pardon . . .

Bert and Ernie Build a Snowman

Here I am, showing my old buddy Bert how to make a BIG snowball.

Now I'm showing Bert how to make a BIGGER snowball.

And now I'm showing Bert how to make the BIGGEST snowball of all.

Here I'm showing Bert how to make a face on the snowman.

And here's our snowman! Pretty good, huh, Bert?

A Day at the Beach — Photos by ERNIE!

Here is a picture of my old buddy BERT and the beautiful sand castle he built. Unfortunately all the picture shows is Bert's LEGS and FEET.

Old Buddy Bert asked me to take a picture of him wearing his super new sunglasses. But most of the picture seems to be Bert's EAR.

Here's Bert swimming. Isn't that a good picture of Bert's HAIR?

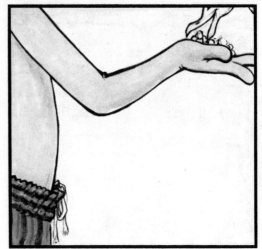

Here's Bert feeding a seagull. It shows what a really nice ELBOW Bert has.

Here's old buddy Bert looking at all the great pictures I took of him. Boy, what a great photo this is of Bert's HEAD! How do you like them, Bert?

**Jack and Jill went up the hill
to fetch a pail of water;**

Jack fell down and broke his crown,
and Jill came tumbling after.

Cookie Monster's Big and Little Cookies

COOKIES GRATIA COO...

You ready for this? This EASIEST recipe of all — you only make two cookies!

A GREAT **BIG** COOKIE like this one...

and a cute, ADORABLE, teeny LITTLE cookie like this one.

You need:
1. COOKIE DOUGH—for this one maybe you better make some more (look at Volume 1).
2. Chocolate chips and crispy rice cereal.

First, roll out dough ¼ inch thick. Now cut out cute LITTLE cookie. O.K.? Now take REST OF DOUGH and cut out **BIGGEST** COOKIE you can fit on cookie sheet. O.K.? Sprinkle chocolate chips and cereal on cookies to make them even MORE delicious. Now put in oven and cook six to eight minutes at 400 degrees.

While you waiting for cookies to cook, you can *color in* PICTURES OF ME and my cookies! That is fun... but it even more fun eating cookies when they're done!

The Shoemaker and the Elves

Once there was a poor old shoemaker who had only enough leather to make one more pair of shoes.

"Let's help him," whispered the elves who hid in his shop. "Let's make the best pair of shoes that anyone ever saw!"

When the tired old shoemaker had gone to bed, the elves came out of their hiding places and made a beautiful pair of shoes. The shoemaker could not figure out where the shoes had come from. But when a rich man bought them the very next day, the shoemaker used the money to buy more leather.

That night the elves returned and made more beautiful shoes. The elves were all over the shop, chuckling and singing at their secret work. The shoemaker woke up and peeked at them. When he saw what was going on, he decided to make tiny new suits for the elves.

The next night the elves found their new suits.

"Thank you very much," they all said. "You are doing so well now that you don't need us any more. But we will come back to visit you every Christmas."

And sure enough, every Christmas the elves did come back, and everyone had a wonderful party.

The Story of Princess Ruby

One day Princess Ruby was out in the garden painting a
picture of her Royal roses. Just as she was painting the last
rose petal, a fox jumped out from behind a rose bush.
Princess Ruby was so startled that she tripped over her chair
and fell right into the bucket of red paint. She had red paint
in her hair, red paint in her ears, and red paint all over her
Royal overalls. She was a mess.

"Blecch!" said Princess Ruby. "I will have to take a bath—and
I've already *had* one today! Oh, I *hate* the color red!"

Princess Ruby went upstairs to the Royal bathtub. Her
mother, Queen Rosalie, took the Royal scrub brush and began
to scrub the Princess. It took an hour to scrub the red paint
off her Royal face. It took another hour to scrub the red
paint out of her Royal hair. It took two more hours to scrub
the red paint out of her Royal ears. And worst of all, her favorite
pair of Royal overalls was ruined!

"Red, red, red! I *hate* the color red! I never want to see the color
red again! Mother," she said, "I want you to issue a Proclamation.
Tell *everyone* in the Kingdom to get rid of EVERYTHING that's red!"

Queen Rosalie, who always tried to please her daughter, said, "All right, dear. But are you sure that's what you want?"

"Absolutely!" shouted Princess Ruby. And so the Queen ordered everyone in the Kingdom to get rid of EVERYTHING that was red.

By now it was dinner time, and Princess Ruby was hungry. She went down to the Royal kitchen and spoke to the Royal cook.

"Royal Cook," she said, "I'm hungry. Make me my favorite sandwich—peanut butter and strawberry jam."

"I am so sorry, Your Highness," said the Royal cook, "but there is no strawberry jam. The Proclamation said we had to get rid of EVERYTHING red, and strawberry jam is red. So out it went! You will have to have peanut butter and mint jelly."

"Yucch!" said the Princess. "Mint jelly is green and disgusting. I *hate* mint jelly."

But that was all there was, so that was what she had.

After dinner it was time for the Princess to go to bed. "Royal Mommy," she said to Queen Rosalie, "will you please read me my favorite bedtime story?"

"Of course, dear," said the Queen. "Which one is that?"

"Oh," said Princess Ruby, "it's the one about the little girl who carries a basket of goodies through the woods to her grandmother's house."

"You mean 'Little Red Riding Hood'?" said the Queen. "We don't have that one any more. You wanted us to get rid of EVERYTHING red, so we had to throw it away. I'll have to read 'Little Boy Blue' instead."

"Aaaacch!" groaned the Princess. "I HATE that story!"

But that was all there was, so that was what she had.

The next day was Valentine's Day, Princess Ruby's favorite day of the year. She LOVED to get valentines. And since everyone in the Kingdom loved *her*, she always got a great many valentines. So, bright and early that morning, she ran down the path to meet the Royal mailman.

"Good morning, Royal Mailman," she said. "May I have my valentines, please?"

"Sorry, Princess," said the mailman, "but valentines are red, and the Proclamation said we had to get rid of EVERYTHING red. So I sent all the valentines to my aunt in Peoria. You'll have to go back and look at that Get Well card I brought you when you had the flu."

"That does it!" yelled the Princess. "Royal Mommy! Royal Mommy! Quick—we need another Proclamation."

"I thought we might," said the Queen, smiling. "I have one right here. I hereby proclaim that the color red is allowed back in the Kingdom!"

And right away, the mailman called his aunt in Peoria and she sent back ALL of Princess Ruby's valentines, AND a big jar of homemade strawberry jam, AND a brand-new copy of "Little Red Riding Hood." And that night, after Ruby had looked at all her valentines and eaten two big peanut butter and strawberry jam sandwiches, and Queen Rosalie had read "Little Red Riding Hood" to her twice, she looked up at her Royal Mommy and said, "Royal Mommy, I've really learned a lesson today. Red is a very important color. My favorite food has red in it, and my favorite story has red in it, and my favorite holiday wouldn't be the same without the color red. In fact, red is my favorite color. From now on I will wear only red overalls, and I will eat only red food, and I only want to hear stories about red things, and I want my room painted red. In fact, I want the whole palace painted red, and..."

Queen Rosalie leaned over, kissed her daughter on the forehead, and said softly, "Yes, dear. Go to sleep now, and we'll talk about it in the morning."

J. Mathieu

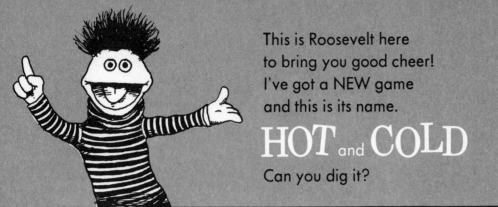

This is Roosevelt here
to bring you good cheer!
I've got a NEW game
and this is its name.

HOT and COLD

Can you dig it?

O.K.
Here's how to play . . .
Get something small—
like a button or a penny. Send your friends out of
the room, and hide it. When you're ready, call your
friends back into the room. Now they have to find it.
They ask you, "Is it near the TV?" If they're close
you say, "You're getting hot." They say, "Is it
under the rug?" If they're further away you
say, "You're getting cold." You keep playing
until someone guesses where it is. Then
that person gets to hide
it next.

MUST be in
the goldfish
bowl!

When you're
hot, you're
hot!

The People in Your Neighborhood

Hi, everybody.
Who are you?

We're People in Your Neighborhood.
See if you can guess which ones we are.

Does your bathtub need repairing?
Is there something in your drain?
Do you have a leaky faucet
That is driving you insane?
Don't call up a policeman—
   that's as silly as can be.
For fixing leaks and tubs and drains
The one to call is ME!
      I am the _ _ _ _ _ _ _ .

When your hair's so long and shaggy
That you bump into a tree,
When you can't see where you're going—
Then it's time to come see ME!
I will cut your hair and comb it,
And I'll make you look so good
That I'll be your very favorite Person
In Your Neighborhood!
      I am the _ _ _ _ _ _ .

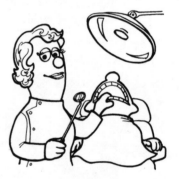

When you come into my office
First you sit down in my chair,
Then you open up your mouth
So I can see the teeth in there.
First I count them—
Then I clean them,
And I see if they're all right,
And I tell you to please brush them
In the morning and at night!
      I am the _ _ _ _ _ _ .

PLUMBER DENTIST BARBER

My Favorite SHAPE!
by Big Bird

The CIRCLE is my favorite shape,
And I will tell you why.
Because it's the shape
Of my FAV-OR-ITE food—
A crunchy birdseed pie!

But...
I mustn't forget the RECTANGLE—
I like *that* best by far.
'Cause that's the shape
Of a *chocolate-covered*
Birdseed candy bar.

But, WAIT! I forgot about TRIANGLES!
Triangles are VERY nice.
Like a piece of birdseed pizza.
Please—can I have a slice?

Oh, no! I can't leave out the SQUARE...
I love that shape the most.
When bedtime comes I always have
Some milk and birdseed toast.

I guess it doesn't matter
If it's round or if it's square—
ALL shapes are really tasty,
So long as BIRDSEED's there.

✒ A BIRD'S TALE ✒

Once upon a time, a long, long time ago, there were two birds who lived together in a little cottage in the woods. The two birds were very good friends...but they didn't know what to call each other. They had no names!

One day the larger bird said to the smaller bird, "Hey! I know! I'm yellow! You can call me Yellow Bird!!"

"That's no good," replied the smaller bird. "I'm

yellow too! If we call you Yellow Bird, what will we call *me*?"

"Oh, that's true," said the large bird. "Well, how about this... I am all covered with feathers. You could call me Feathery Bird!"

"I have feathers too," said the small bird. "That's no good."

"Well, how about my feet?" said the large bird. "You could call me Orange-Feet-With-Three-Toes! How would *that* be?"

"I have orange feet with three toes also," said the small bird sadly.

"What about calling me Bird-With-Big-Googly-Eyes-and-A-Beak-Instead-Of-A-Nose-With-A-Red-Hat!" suggested the large bird.

The small bird sighed. "I have big googly eyes and I have a beak instead of a nose... and there's my red hat hanging over there on the hook."

"Oh, dear," said the large bird. "We seem to be exactly the same in every way. We'll just have to have the same name, too. There is absolutely nothing at all to tell us apart."

"Except that you're so big and I'm so little," said the small bird.

"That's it!" yelled the large bird. "I'm big and you're little!! That's the answer!! We'll call me... Great Huge Enormous Bird... and we'll call you... Wee Tiny Small Bird!"

"How's about just Big Bird and Little Bird, huh?"

Hey, Bert, did you notice that picture of us in this book? The one with the terrific snowman we made?
Ernie